ANCIENT GHOSTS

A COLLECTION OF STRANGE AND SCARY STORIES FROM NORTHERN NORWAY

WRITTEN BY
Edel Marit Gaino

ILLUSTRATED BY
Toma Feizo Gas

TRANSLATED FROM NORTH SÁMI BY
Olivia Lasky and Lea Simma

Table of Contents

The Old Graves on Our Moor

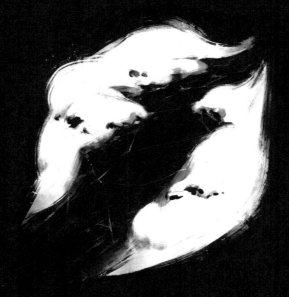

Uncle Niillas was the kind of person who liked to read books about strange scientific discoveries. My uncle was a very tall man—so tall that he had to crouch down when he came through the door.

"Listen to this," he said. "They found an ancient corpse in a bog in Denmark—and it hasn't even decomposed! It's been there for thousands of years and still has all of his clothes and tools. The bog preserved it like ice. It seems he'd been tortured before he was put in the bog."

He showed me a picture of an ugly man who looked like he was made entirely of darkened tendon. I didn't like looking at it, but I was old enough to at least try to act tough, so I carefully studied the images in the book. My eyes stopped on one particularly gruesome photo: the bog corpse was wrinkled like old leather. *Horrifying*, I thought.

Uncle Niillas was always quite serious when he talked about this kind of thing.

Scientists had been to our village in the past and marked the old graves on our **moor**. I don't think my uncle liked that they had disturbed them. But can you imagine? There were old graves just outside that we walked past every day!

Stones had been placed side by side in a circle. Uncle Niillas told me about how the scientists had a method that used carbon to determine the age of the bones underground. They were ancient graves, and we kids were absolutely *not* allowed to go anywhere near them. They were not to be disturbed. We knew where each of the old graves was, and playing there was strictly forbidden.

Ráimmahallan—what did it mean? Being scared of ghosts? We'd heard of it, but we didn't really understand it. Whatever it was, it sounded terrifying.

During the dark winter months, I'd sometimes pass the moor on my way home to avoid the crack in the ice on the creek. My friends lived on the other side of the creek, and normally they would walk me part of the way back. One time in particular, though, they didn't come with me.

5

I was terrified of walking alone in the dark. I tried to see if I could spot the lights from our house beyond the moor and decided I would cross the frozen creek to save time. It wasn't covered in snow yet, so I took careful steps on the slippery black ice. I could see straight through it in the moonlight. I spotted bubbles and seaweed moving along the creek bed by the banks. I lit the way with my flashlight. I was truly quite scared of crossing the creek like this, but it was so much faster than walking all the way around. I was terrified but tried to stay tough and quickened my steps so I could get home as fast as possible.

That's when I slipped. My head hit the ice—hard. I heard a strange echoing sound and saw lights flash before my eyes. I lay there all alone. No one had seen me. I was almost knocked out cold.

I couldn't get up or even make a sound. I just lay there, my head throbbing. The stars in the sky above me seemed like they were spinning round and round when I finally managed to open my eyes.

Apparently, someone *had* seen me, though, because suddenly there was someone beside me. I hadn't even heard anyone come. They were completely silent, and I couldn't see who it was in the dark. All I could tell was they were really, *really* big. My eyelids were still flickering, and I couldn't see all that well yet. I felt the person's fur coat shedding slightly as they lifted me up by my shoulders, and the fur—or something like fur, at least—blew all over my face.

"Uncle Niillas, I swear I had permission to cross the creek!" I cried. I worried I would get in trouble for crossing the ice by myself. At the same time, I wondered why he was wearing these strange clothes.

He didn't say anything as he lifted me on his back and started

walking toward our house. The world was still spinning, and I huddled up against his back so he wouldn't slip on the ice while carrying me.

We were almost back at our moor, and I could see the lights from our house close by. But then he stopped abruptly and set me down. My head was still spinning, and I tried to keep my balance so I wouldn't fall.

He took my hand, and I was startled by how dry it was—like rotten, wrinkled leather! I looked up at him and couldn't quite see his face, but I could see that he was much, much older than me. It was dark with only the moon shining dimly above. He'd stopped right at the old graves on our moor.

I got scared and ran back to the house as fast as possible, not daring to look back. Who was he? What kind of strange person was that?

I got inside as quickly as I could—safe and sound! Mama and Uncle Niillas were eating in the kitchen. I stared out the window with big round eyes but didn't see anyone standing on the moor in the moonlight. Who was my silent helper? Who was that person who wouldn't go beyond the old graves on the moor?

Mama and Uncle Niillas thought I was probably seeing things, since I had hit my head so hard. I had a big wound on the back of my head, and Mama blew on it through my wool hat to help it heal.

But first, she had to brush off my hat—it was covered in **reindeer** hair, like I'd been rolling around on an old fur.

8

The Copper Kettle

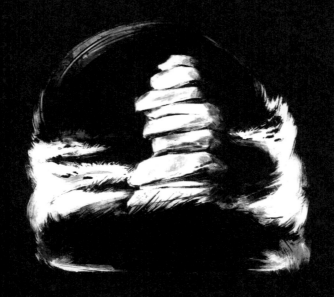

It was late fall, and the village farmers still had a lot of work left to do before winter. About half a day's trip from the village was a place called Goddejeaggi—wild reindeer bog. North of the bog was a place called Goddejávri—wild reindeer lake. This lake was full of strong, stout fish. There weren't any measly perch or pike—just big, fat whitefish the farmers would catch with nets. The leaves around Goddejávri had started yellowing, and you could spot a few frostbitten cloudberries on the mounds. Lingonberries shone red on the hills.

Three good friends—brothers Máhtte and Joavnna and their cousin Ovllá—were in a tractor, driving to Goddejeaggi. The brothers sat stretched out in the trailer while Ovllá drove carefully along the rocky tractor path. There were quite a few trapping pits in the area around Goddejeaggi, and he really didn't want to get stuck in one or have any mishaps in the forest. They finally made it to Goddejeaggi unharmed.

The boys thought there was something a bit eerie about Goddejeaggi that day, but they had arrived in the evening, after all, and it got dark quickly this time of year. They'd set up a camp the last time they were here just a few weeks ago, but they couldn't find it now. It was almost as though someone was trying to play a prank on them by moving the stones they'd used to make a fireplace. They were also a bit nervous about encountering the bear that had left tracks in the area earlier, during cloudberry season.

They made a new camp in a spot that seemed suitable enough. Perhaps it was even the same place as before, but they couldn't see that well in the dark.

"It's so strange that our fireplace would just disappear like that. I'm going to go have a look around," said Máhtte, the oldest of the three.

He headed off, taking a flashlight with him, since he didn't like the idea of stumbling around in the dark near the bog in case he happened to fall into a mudhole.

He shone his light around and spotted a large pile of stones. *Some Norwegians must have taken the stones from the fireplace and put them here so they wouldn't get lost*, he thought. Someone had stacked the flat stones from the fireplace one on top of the other. He wondered why they'd been stacked so high right next to this small pit. They were rough, grey stones on which moss and other vegetation had made some faint images.

"Now we can make a fire," Ovllá said when Máhtte returned. He had already collected some dry firewood. Máhtte placed the flat stones in a circle to make a fireplace, and just a few minutes later, the wood had burst into flames.

Now they could finally have a cup of evening coffee! They were exhausted, and the only thing left to do was lie down and sleep. They really had found a nice campsite.

Ovllá and Joavnna fell asleep quickly, but Máhtte stayed awake, thinking about the pile of stones at the pit. He looked at the fireplace, the light of the flames flickering against a stone with a sooty black coffee pot sitting on top of it. There was still some coffee left in it, and when Máhtte picked it up to pour himself a cup, he noticed some lines in the stone: it looked like someone had carved the letter X.

I knew that was no ordinary pile of stones! Máhtte thought, pulling on his boots and grabbing his flashlight. He had to go back to take a closer look.

It was quiet and very dark. He shone his flashlight on the pit where the pile of stones was. There was something genuinely creepy about it, but he didn't know why he had such an uneasy feeling. Still, he shone the flashlight between the stones, feeling he simply had to investigate. Were there more stones with carvings? Then Máhtte caught a glimpse of something glittering at the bottom of the pile. He started picking up the stones one by one. They were heavy and thudded against one another as he tossed them aside.

After some time, he could see what was under all those stones: a beautiful copper kettle. He picked it up, and something inside rattled. Máhtte practically flung the lid open. He'd found an old treasure! Inside were darkened silver coins, a square silver button, and a silver chain. He shone his flashlight into the pit to see if there was more treasure down there, but he saw nothing besides dirt and heather.

Máhtte took the copper kettle back to their campsite to show his friends how rich they were now! Museums would pay a lot for this kind of treasure. Even though he lived out in the forest, he knew that much. As he was walking, he kept looking over his shoulder from time to time as though he'd stolen something and was afraid of getting caught.

He laid the silver out on a reindeer skin to study the coins more closely, but he couldn't tell how old they were. *You can look at them tomorrow in the daylight,* he thought as he put everything back in the kettle. *The boys aren't going to believe their eyes!* He smiled as he lay back down. But no matter how hard he tried, he simply couldn't fall asleep. He twisted and turned, but he just couldn't get comfortable. He stared at the glowing embers and eventually fell asleep.

Máhtte started dreaming. Or...was it a dream? He heard a scraping noise against the fabric of the tent, almost as though someone was dragging their sharp nails across it. There wasn't even a breath of wind, though—what could it be? First he could hear the sound along the side of the tent, and then it moved past the sitting area by the fireplace before it continued toward the doorway. Could it be a *muodd'áddjá*—a brown bear—that was looking for a way in? The tent door flew open as though there had been a strong gust of

wind. Máhtte lay completely still, squeezing his eyes shut. He felt a cloud of ash hit his face and smoke blow into his nose, making his throat sting. But he couldn't cough. It just got harder and harder for him to breathe. He felt a weight on his feet at first; then he couldn't move at all. Was the bear stepping on him? But if it was a bear, wouldn't it be growling? He couldn't see anything in the pitch dark. He tried to play dead, since he'd heard that's what you should do if a bear starts attacking you.

It started getting even harder to breathe, as though something was pressing on his chest. Máhtte could hear something strange— like stones hitting one another as someone piled them on top of him. If he'd been able to move, the stones would've fallen off of him, but it was as if he was paralyzed. He couldn't move a muscle. It was like he'd been sewn onto the reindeer hide. Behind him, he could hear the kettle fall over and the silver clinking loudly next to his ear. Why weren't Joavnna and Ovllá waking up to help him?

Máhtte's heart was pounding. Sweat poured down his face, and it felt like his life was flowing out of him. What evil had put this on him? *I'm going to pass out*, he thought, fearing for his life. Then everything went black.

He woke up when Ovllá and Joavnna started shaking him.

"Wake up! Wake up!" they shouted in a panic. "You scare us when you snort in your sleep like that! Are you sick or something?" They looked at Máhtte's swollen, red face. "Were you having a nightmare?"

"The copper kettle! Where is it?" Máhtte looked at the spot where he'd put the kettle last night, but it was gone. He could practically hear the kettle filled with silver rattling in his ears. He pulled on his boots and rushed back to the place he'd gone last night. His two friends hurried after him.

The stones were stacked neatly on top of one another by the pit, untouched. Máhtte started picking them up and flinging them aside. "There was a copper kettle full of silver here last night! You have to see!" he said.

Suddenly, he grabbed a sharp piece of bone that was lying between the stones. It went straight into his hand! He could no longer dig and had to wrap up his hand to stop it from bleeding. That's when he understood what it was that he had found: he'd disturbed an old tomb and taken grave markers as rocks for the fireplace. If only he had known!

The old man—*ájján*—flaunted both his riches and his powers that night. He wasn't playing around when he scared Máhtte just as much as a *muodd'áddjá* would have.

The three friends never would have gotten rich from that copper kettle. After this experience, Máhtte was certain of that much.

The Grouse

It was quiet on the remote campground. Smoke rose from the chimney of the cabin where a young woman named Biret had just lit a fire in the wood stove. She looked out the window. She was spending yet another fall taking care of the forest cabins here, cooking and cleaning for the grouse hunters. The pay was decent, and she liked meeting all different kinds of people. Biret pulled her long jet-black hair into a ponytail. She was very beautiful, meticulous, and well prepared for the guests' arrival. Everything was clean and tidy.

Will the hunters be arriving soon? Biret wondered, thinking about the group of men who had booked the cabin.

They usually came with their birding dogs and ATVs every fall and rented a cabin in the area. They were a fun, rowdy bunch—and Biret thought that at least one of them was pretty handsome. Imagine if he came this year as well!

Biret started daydreaming about the kind, outdoorsy Norwegian she'd developed a bit of a crush on.

But does he even remember me? Biret really hoped so.

Now it was just a matter of waiting. There was no Internet, and you had to go to the top of the hill nearby if you wanted to make a call. Other people took summer jobs at hotels and restaurants and such in the village, but Biret longed to be in nature. She felt safe here, and it was such a peaceful place! She wasn't at all afraid of being alone in the wilderness.

The hours passed, and the guests still hadn't arrived. Biret thought this was strange, since they had been supposed to arrive earlier that day. She didn't know if she should start cooking dinner or not, so she got dressed and started walking up the hill, in case they'd sent a text that they would be delayed.

She held her phone up in the air and waited for a signal. She stood there for a while, enjoying the view, although she couldn't see that far. She hadn't gotten to the top yet, and there were still quite a few leaves on the trees in the dense fall forest. She couldn't see the house from where she was standing and decided to climb up a bit higher to get a better view.

She hadn't gone far when something strange happened: she heard a sound, and a speckled grouse landed right next to her at full speed! She tried to run away, but the grouse kept flapping around her, jumping in front of her and trying to force its way between her legs.

This is crazy! she thought. The grouse's behaviour was so bizarre that Biret didn't know what to do. She just stood there, waiting to see what would happen.

She heard a shriek coming from the sky—perhaps a falcon, considering attacking the grouse? Biret couldn't think of any other explanation but wasn't able to see if it actually was a falcon in the air through the thick canopy of trees. The terrible screech felt like it was slicing through her body.

The grouse kept Biret from continuing up or down the hill. She tried to move sideways, but it just squawked even louder.

What a noise! Biret covered her ears.

"Damn grouse, leave me alone!" she shouted.

Her phone was completely useless without a signal, but who could she call anyway, and what would she even say? That she was being chased by a grouse? It seemed so utterly absurd.

It started getting dark. All of a sudden, the grouse hopped between the dwarf birches and disappeared. Biret sprinted back toward the cabins like she was being chased to her death. The grouse had really spooked her. Who would believe her if she told them about this? Absolutely no one!

She was getting closer to the log cabin when she got a strange feeling. She stopped, as though she could sense something. She heard the sound of breaking glass and some men shouting.

Two ATVs Biret didn't recognize were parked outside the house.

She snuck up to peek inside. A candle was burning, and she could see the shadows of two strange men moving around. They had broken some plates, and one of them was smashing a chair to pieces on the floor.

These were dangerous men—roaring drunk and making a complete mess of the cabin. But they hadn't gotten what they'd really come for: a young woman.

Biret ran. The grouse! The grouse had warned her. Now she understood its strange behaviour. It wanted to keep her from being at home when these dangerous men were on the hunt. They surely would have forced themselves on her if she'd been at home! She hid until the men drove away.

Animals can have premonitions, especially for people who have a close relationship with nature and all creatures. That's what saved Biret.

The Mudhole

A young girl named Gáren was standing on a tall mound at the edge of the moor, studying something carefully. She had spotted a shimmering, flowing liquid—she didn't realize she'd come across quicksilver!

If only I could get closer! she thought. She was well aware that this was a moor you could easily sink into. She found a stick to try to reach it, but without success.

If I hop onto the next mound, I can get to it! Gáren thought. She balanced on the edge of the mound, the swamp right in front of her. Deep in the mudhole, the quicksilver seemed to be swirling in the water like the northern lights.

Suddenly, she heard someone shouting from a bit farther away. "Don't get anywhere near that terrible mudhole!"

Who was that? She couldn't see anyone! She was so startled she slipped off the mound, grabbing at a dwarf birch as she fell.

"Mama!" she cried.

But her mother wasn't there—she was picking cloudberries, too far away to hear.

Gáren screamed, feeling herself sinking into the mudhole. The more she kicked and struggled, the more she got stuck. No matter how hard she tried to climb back onto the mound, she couldn't get a good foothold with her moccasins.

I'm never going to get back up! she thought, terrified. She tried desperately to grab onto the few twigs and branches of heather she could reach. She felt the rotten twigs breaking off between her fingers and the heather coming loose from the ground no matter where she grabbed it.

Quicksilver lures children to their deaths. Gáren was so taken by the beauty of the shimmering liquid that she forgot to watch out for the bottomless mudhole.

When cloudberry pickers passed by this place much later, they would neither see nor understand the terrible thing that had happened here.

A child had sunk deep into the swamp of death and disappeared while cloudberry picking a long, long time ago. She never got the chance to know who had called out to her. It was probably a child the mudhole had also lured into another world.

This is why it's important to teach children about how dangerous mudholes can be.

The Mirror

It was New Year's Eve, and two teenage girls were reading their horoscopes in a magazine. What would happen in the coming year?

"Do you believe in this kind of thing?" Janne looked at Máret, a serious expression on her face. "Do you believe in astrology?"

Máret wasn't the kind of person who believed in **divination**. She thought that horoscopes and tarot cards were just nonsense.

"Not really, but they're fun to read. Listen to this." She read what was going to happen to Virgos when it came to romance. Janne was a Virgo. "*This year, dear Virgo, you must travel somewhere with a lot of people. This is where you will meet the love of your life. It might be an unexpected person—perhaps even someone you've never noticed before!*"

Hmm...who could it be? The girls giggled and thought about the boys they'd never really paid much attention to. Could it be that Norwegian guy? No, not him! He didn't talk about anything except computer games. He couldn't even flirt if he tried. They laughed the way teenage girls do.

"But he *is* really nice to girls," Máret said.

"Let's read your horoscope, too," Janne said. "What does it say?" They flipped to Máret's star sign—Gemini. "Okay, Gemini," Janne began. "*You must be careful when it comes to love. Don't fall so head over heels that you go crazy and can no longer see the truth.*"

"Hmmm," Máret said, suddenly very serious.

Janne quickly tried to find a more optimistic prediction. "Listen to this, then: *If you're single, you'll meet someone who is spiritual and who will give you a new perspective on life!* Well, that's good, at least! Think about it: you'll meet a priest and be a priestess by this time next year!"

They burst out laughing again. They really were having a lot of fun! Then, Janne remembered a trick you can do on New Year's Eve.

"Should we try something I heard about?" Janne asked.

Janne went to get Máret's gold mirror from the bathroom and

set it down on the table in the living room. Máret stared into it, wondering what tricks Janne had up her sleeve this time.

"You have to look into the mirror right at midnight—and you'll see your future boyfriend," Janne said, smiling mischievously.

They sat down on the couch, and Janne turned the mirror so they could both see their faces. It was a few minutes to 12. Soon the fireworks would start going off outside.

The mirror reflected a few fireworks that the neighbours were setting off early. The big window in the living room was right behind the couch, so the mirror also showed the reflection of the dark courtyard.

"Are we really going to do this?" Máret asked. "What if it actually shows someone? What do we do then? Do you *have* to be with that person just because the mirror showed them?" She didn't believe in astrology, but she *was* a little bit afraid of this kind of thing.

"I don't know. I've never tried it. But it's just for fun, right?" Janne decided they should just do it.

Máret was a bit unsure. Did she dare look in the mirror when the clock struck 12? "Ahh, we're just playing around, I guess," she said after a moment.

They emptied their glasses of soda. Soon, it would be time to see what the mirror showed. Soon, they would see their fates in the mirror. Who would they marry?

The clock ticked, approaching midnight. More and more fireworks started going off outside. The girls fell silent. They didn't even say "Happy New Year" to each other—they just stared at the mirror.

Máret's eyes were glued to the mirror, but she saw only her own reflection. Janne was also looking, staring straight into her own eyes. She didn't dare look away.

Máret thought about the new year and all the possibilities that came with it. Every now and then, she could see the reflection of the fireworks flashing through the living room window. Everything sparkled green and yellow. Then she looked at Janne's reflection: she was white as a sheet! Her eyes seemed to be fixed on something she couldn't tear her gaze away from, even when Máret spoke to her.

"Janne, what is it?! Hello? I didn't see anything. What are you looking at?"

Máret touched her friend's shoulder—and then Janne started screaming at the top of her lungs, like she'd been scared half to death. It was terrifying to see how pale Janne had gotten in an instant.

"What did you see? Tell me!" Máret demanded.

"Did you not see what I saw?" Janne whispered.

What was she talking about? Janne seemed too serious to be joking around. Máret said she hadn't seen anything except herself and the fireworks outside.

"What did you see?" Máret suddenly got a bad feeling in her stomach.

"I...can't say it! Never!" Janne really didn't seem to be kidding....

"Can't you tell me?" Máret waited for her friend to answer her.

But Janne stayed silent. Each time she tried to say something, it was like the words got stuck in her throat. She couldn't say anything because secret forces were controlling her.

31

"Did you see the fireworks?" Máret asked.

Janne didn't answer.

"Did you see yourself?"

Janne nodded. "Yes, at first, but then...My tongue can't seem to make the words! Why?" Janne looked at her friend fearfully and grabbed her hands. "I love you so much. You're my best friend. Never forget that! Goodness always triumphs over evil. Remember that!"

She never talked like this. Máret thought it was strange, not to mention scary.

"Did you see the fireworks in the mirror?" Máret wanted to know what Janne had seen.

"No...it was completely dark, and..." Tears started streaming down her face, and she could no longer speak. "I need to go home now!"

She left in a hurry, and Máret put the mirror back in the bathroom. It was a nice antique she'd bought the year before.

Máret felt anxious. Did she dare call and ask what had happened? They'd been having so much fun, but now she just felt sick to her stomach. It was like it had all been a nightmare.

The next day, Máret and Janne went on a long walk. They agreed they'd never do this kind of thing again. They wouldn't believe in or trust divination. Fate was something only *they* had control over. They shouldn't believe everything they read in magazines, and they would never try any kind of magic like this again.

Back at home, Máret jumped into the shower. She and Janne had walked until they were sweaty.

The hot steam from the shower filled the bathroom, and Máret never saw the invisible finger that drew a star in the mirror. No one had touched it since the night before. There was no point in trying to clean it. No matter what, the star would always appear after a shower. Máret ended up having to call a spiritual helper to cleanse the entire house after the incident on New Year's Eve.

The Raven

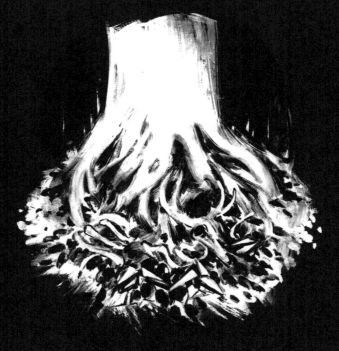

My friend experienced something a long time ago that left such an impression on him that it still affects him to this day. Ole lives in Varanger and is the kind of person who can survive in the wilderness—an adventurous man. He isn't afraid of thick, dark forests, and he used to go grouse hunting every fall.

Ole talks about the experience like this: "I wanted to test out a shotgun I'd borrowed, since I was planning on using it for hunting grouse a few weeks later. I thought that if it was a good shotgun, I might even try to buy it from the owner. I couldn't shoot a weapon too close to the houses, though, so I went out to a deserted area that I didn't know all that well.

"I stopped the car, and my dog leaped out as fast as he could. He was a hyper young birding dog, but he was obedient, so I let him run off.

"I looked through the scope of the shotgun and could see a raven on top of a pine tree a couple hundred metres away. My dog had spotted it as well, stopping to look up at it. He started to growl a little, and when I looked through the scope, I could see that the bird was ugly and strangely large for a raven. There was a big rock at the base of the pine tree that almost looked like it had fallen straight down from the sky. *Soon this raven will also fall to the earth*, I thought.

"I let the dog run over to scare the raven out of the tree, and he bounded off. It wasn't a grouse, but this dog breed goes crazy for all kinds of birds. The raven flapped its wings and took off, and I fired! I hit it and watched it fall through the branches and down to the ground like a black sail.

"It seemed like the gun had pretty good aim, since I was able to hit the bird from so far away. I triumphantly made my way toward the pine tree and the rock where the bird had fallen. The dog ran ahead to sniff the bird's blood.

"Suddenly, he started whining as though he'd been whipped! I saw him cowering and licking his front paw. I hurried closer and saw that the poor thing was covered in blood! His front paw was wounded—what had cut it?

"The bird had fallen into a cleft in the rock where there were sharp bones, horns, and shards of glass on the ground. When I saw that, I decided we should head straight home before something else happened to my dog!

"'Come on, pup!' I said, but it seemed like he almost didn't dare move. He limped a few steps and then whined some more. I realized I had no choice but to carry him back to the car. As I started to walk, I could hear something cawing behind me. It looked like there was a second raven back there, and it seemed aggressive.

"I glanced back and saw that this creature was about to attack me! It was flying directly at me, and since I had a dog in my arms and a heavy weapon on my back, I wouldn't be able to shoot it. I started running back to the car as fast as I could. The raven screeched horribly as it flapped above me. I ducked down just as it came straight at my eyes.

"'Get away, devil!' I shouted.

"I was out of breath as I put the dog in the back of the car. I barely got in myself before the raven landed on the hood and started flapping its wings like the devil himself had sent it after me.

"My dog was never the same after that. He growled all the time and even snapped at the vet when they were trying to examine his foot. He would always bite people after this, and I unfortunately had to put him down."

I remembered what I'd heard about ravens. They often settle in spots where people had places of worship. These kinds of places had often witnessed violent, brutal fights where people had been killed. Many believed the raven was an unlucky bird. There was no

point in having bad thoughts about it, though—because you might end up getting into an accident and limping forever.

That's probably why things went so poorly for my friend Ole's dog. Sometimes he still thinks about that black bird that attacked him and almost pecked out his eyes so he wouldn't be able to see or shoot ever again.

The Dream-Seers

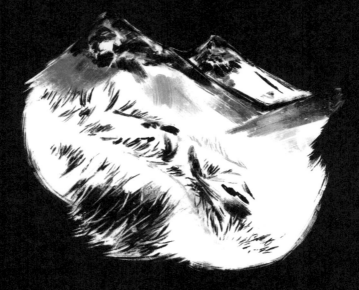

When you are a dream-seer, you often have dreams about things that are going to happen—things that you might not truly understand until they happen in reality. Sometimes the dream is so vivid that you remember it quite clearly when you wake up. If you tell someone who is good at reading dreams, they might be able to help you interpret it. It's common to interpret dreams among our people, and it can be both a joy and a nuisance for the dreamer. We often experience dreams that have messages we don't understand until much later.

I once dreamt that I was walking along a mountain trail on a beautiful day. I heard a familiar voice behind me. My *áhkku*—my grandmother—had said my name! My áhkku had passed away a long time ago, but I didn't seem to know that in the dream. I looked back and saw her smiling at me. She asked, "Where are you going?"

"That way," I said, pointing north.

I looked at the tall mountains in front of me, the kind you usually see along the coast.

"I can walk with you for a bit," said my áhkku. "You don't have much farther to go."

Áhkku stood next to me and pointed at the valley stretching out in front of us. There was an incredibly beautiful green meadow filled with yellow flowers. "You should go there!" she said and then left. She headed south, where we'd come from.

I made my way down to the meadow. There was a stream with a lovely pure-white sandy beach and water so clear you could see the salmon swimming upstream. When I went over to the beach, I saw something at the bottom of the stream that caught my attention. I wondered what it was and waded out. It wasn't all that deep. The water was up to my knees when I made a terrible discovery.

There was a man lying there. He was chained to a large rock at the bottom of the stream. I wasn't afraid, though, and carried the poor man up to the beach. I shouted for help, but no one could hear me.

Then I woke up and wondered what the dream meant.

A few months later, I got to know a person who hid their dark side. Had the dream perhaps come as a warning for me not to get

into situations that would be bad for me? I'll never know.

Perhaps the dream meant that my ancestors were trying to make me aware that I would be facing an important event in my life. "Be careful, dear descendants," it seemed to warn.

I've never forgotten that dream—because it came true.

The Four-Eyed Dog

I've always thought of dogs as incredibly intelligent animals. You can teach them all kinds of tricks and commands and communicate with them.

Dogs have particularly acute vision and hearing, and their sense of smell is almost too powerful for their own good! But some dogs also have strange gifts that humans can't quite understand. This kind of dog is something like an "in-between person"—

someone who sees and hears what others don't. A bit like a shaman, perhaps.

These dogs have a small mark over each eye, so it almost looks like they have four eyes. I've heard stories about these special four-eyed dogs that always astonish me.

There was a reindeer herder who managed to get lost as he was heading home one day. It had gotten dark, and there was a frosty mist hovering in the air, making it difficult to see. He was driving his snowmobile and was lucky to come across an old cabin deep in the forest. He stopped outside and considered sleeping there. After all, he didn't want to find himself even farther off course.

He had his dog with him—a smart old dog who seemed to understand almost anything you said to him. He was black except for the light marks over both eyes. That's why he was named Čálmmo—since he looked like he had an extra set of eyes.

"This is a special dog," people would say. "He can see more than what we see."

"Alright, Čálmmo," the man said. "I guess we'll shack up here for the night." The dog hopped off the snowmobile.

The man had to kick his way through the deep snow to get to the cabin door. The door had a rusty doorknob but no keyhole, just a kind of hook to open it.

A few dented water jugs were hanging from some big, rusty nails on the wall in the entry.

But Čálmmo wouldn't go in. The man called him again and again, but the stubborn dog just kept whining outside. Eventually, the man left the front door open and went further into the

47

darkness. There was only one room in the cabin, and he could barely see anything at all.

There were some cups and candles on a small table at the other end of the room. The man lit a candle and spotted a wood stove in the corner. There was also a rusty iron bed without a mattress. God only knows how old that bed was. He must have come across a German cabin from wartime.

"Good thing there's some dry wood here so we can light a fire!" the man said. The dog had now come a bit farther into the entryway and was peeking in through the door.

"Come on in, pup!" the man said, patting his thigh so the dog would come to him. Čálmmo finally obeyed and came inside. He sniffed what seemed like every inch of the place before finally lying down next to his owner, who was trying to get the fire started.

"I need to shut the door so we can keep warm in here," the man said as he pulled the door shut.

It was getting nice and warm in the cabin, and the candle flickered prettily in the semi-darkness. The man set the kettle on the stove to boil, looking forward to a hot cup of coffee.

After he was done eating, he put his rucksack on the floor to use as a pillow and lay on his side in the circle of warmth cast by the stove. He was a bit concerned by how uneasy and restless Čálmmo was. The dog didn't even want to eat. He just sniffed at the crusts of bread on the ground and peered at the front door, his ears rigid and alert. He kept looking from the window to the door as though he were looking at something outside.

The man stared at the dog. Could he hear something? Or was he seeing something the man couldn't?

Then, Čálmmo started to growl. He got up and stood between the man and the door, his hackles raised. It was quite creepy, actually—what on Earth was he sensing? Čálmmo was now growling so much that the man stood up as well. What if there was a murderer or something out there?

"Who's out there?" he shouted.

There wasn't any answer, but the man heard some scratching noises coming from the entryway. Something was scraping against the water jugs! Čálmmo was now snarling like he'd completely lost his mind. He would protect his master at all costs, and one must be careful around an agitated dog! Čálmmo's sharp white teeth shone in the candlelight when he growled.

Suddenly, the door opened with so much force that it slammed against the wall like it had been shot open with a rifle. The candle went out and the room went pitch black—but no one came in, and there wasn't a gust of wind to be heard!

The man decided right then and there that it would be foolish to stay. He grabbed his rucksack and hurried out the door with the frightened dog. They hopped on the snowmobile and sped off, leaving a spray of snow behind them.

That cabin is still there. No one ever tried to stay the night there again. The man slammed the door shut behind him as he left, so whatever it was that was haunting it would be trapped inside.

Perhaps Čálmmo had seen a devil from wartime—and that's who he'd been protecting his master from.

The Invisible Dog

I am a mother. My boy came first, and then two years later, I had a little girl. I love to watch how children develop and how they slowly learn to speak. My son, Jonas, was always quick to repeat new words as he learned them, but he'd also say some words the way children who are just a couple of years old do. A bird was "tweet-tweet," and a dog was of course "woof-woof"—and that's how he played around with words.

It was the middle of winter, and I was pregnant with my second child when I witnessed something I still can't explain.

Jonas was sleeping in the big bed I shared with my husband while the two of us were in the living room watching a movie. It was late, and I turned off the TV before getting up to brush my teeth. Just as I was about to squeeze out some toothpaste, the lights started to flicker.

Was there something going on with the electricity? I stood in the bathroom in my nightgown. It wasn't the first time the lights had flickered in this house, but then the lights went out entirely.

"Can you get a flashlight?" I called out to my husband. I was getting nervous because it was pitch black in the bathroom.

As I waited, I felt something touch my foot, almost like a dog was sniffing me—but we didn't have a dog! I was terrified, and my heart was pounding. What on Earth was there? My husband finally came with a flashlight, and I didn't tell him what had happened. I was afraid he'd only laugh at me.

The power was out and neither of us knew why. "Nothing else to do but get cozy under the covers when it's so dark in the house," I said.

I opened the bedroom door. To our shock, when we shone the flashlight at the bed, we saw Jonas kneeling there, staring into a dark corner with big round eyes.

"Woof! Woof!" he kept saying, pointing at the corner.

I shone the flashlight where he was pointing, and that's when the strangest thing happened: Jonas got up in bed, and it really seemed like he was seeing something we couldn't! He stretched out

his arms like he was letting a dog sniff him, but he stood firmly, like he was making sure it didn't suddenly knock him over the way some bigger dogs do.

Jonas kept pointing, laughing, and saying, "Woof." He was staring at the wall on the other side of the room as though the "woof" was about to bound straight through it!

I tried to ask him what he could see and where it was going.

"Woof!" he said. Then he lay down and fell back asleep.

I was still in awe. Was he having a nightmare?

A few years later, Jonas's little sister, Mia, was almost two when something strange happened once again. Mia was also a talkative child. It was just after Christmas, and as is always the case during the dark winter months, it was quite easy to put the two children to bed. We were in the same room where Jonas had seen the invisible dog before.

Jonas fell asleep right away, but Mia wouldn't stop tossing and turning. I pretended I was sleeping in the hope that she would settle down. Suddenly, I heard her laughing.

"Woof! Over there!" she said.

My eyes flew open. Mia was pointing at the same corner Jonas had two years before, and she was also saying there was a dog over there! It was so creepy in the semi-darkness that I turned on the light. But again, I didn't see a dog in the room. It seemed like Mia only saw the dog for a moment before it disappeared, because she fell asleep not long after.

I then understood that we apparently *did* have a dog, and that it protected us in this room. It was a kind dog, and sometimes it even revealed itself to the children. When they got older, the children didn't see or mention it anymore, but I knew that it was still in our house.

Young children's senses of perception are much more open, which is why they don't question things that would seem unbelievable to adults.

The Fishing Trip

I'm heading out for a fishing trip. I like being alone, and now I'm making my way at my own pace, lost in my thoughts as I head down an old tractor trail to the forest. I haven't been here by myself for a long time, but somehow it doesn't really feel like I'm completely alone anyway. I look at the dense, dark woods, and I don't dare stay there long. I suddenly get chills running down my spine, and the hair on the back of my neck stands up. I pick up the pace and try to avert my eyes from that haunted-looking forest. There's a lake behind the hill over there where there should be an upside-down rotten old boat. I vaguely remember it being where the path makes a turn, and my eyes scan for it.

Where is that boat? I wonder. I used to know this area like the back of my hand, but now I hardly even recognize it. I look behind me and spot some crooked black birches on a low hill, but otherwise, there's nothing to be seen.

I'm not normally this scared! *Is it because I'm alone?* I wonder. *Or perhaps because it's getting dark?* I decide right then and there that I'm not going to be afraid of this nonsense.

The sun is just setting behind a hill. *Now I won't worry about anything besides catching a big trout!* I think.

I might catch the biggest one at dawn if I choose the right bait. I get to the beach. *Aha, there's the rotten boat!* I smile. At least I always end up finding the right path! The boat had once belonged to an old man, and no one had taken care of it or tarred it for ages. I walk around it, examining it carefully. Willow branches have grown through the gaps between the boards, which have cracks everywhere. I pull it to the edge of the beach. It's still quite sturdy. There's a fishing net holder on the bow that's also rotted. It doesn't seem like anyone's been to this beach for a very long time. There aren't any fish scales on the flat stones usually used for fish cleaning. *Why not?* I wonder. *Why doesn't anyone set nets in a lake where so many fish feed so close to the surface?*

I take off my boots and start wading in the water along the beach. The water is so warm!

I take off all my clothes. I know I'm alone, so no one can see me. I've been walking so fast that I'm sweating. It's going to feel so good, and I can swim naked in peace!

The water is lukewarm against my skin, but it gets colder the farther out I wade. I stir up the mud with my feet. Brown sand and debris from the bottom swirl around my toes. I keep wading until the water reaches my stomach and I can no longer see my feet. The bottom drops off suddenly in front of me, and I start getting nervous. I'm not much of a swimmer, and if I take another step, I'll sink!

I take a step back and stumble a bit on a slippery, algae-covered rock on the bottom. I flail my arms to keep myself upright. It feels like the drop-off is pulling me to the bottom!

"Oh no, I'm sinking!" I cry out.

I swallow muddy water in a panic and feel the cold from the deeper water against the base of my head. I manage to get a foothold on the bottom again and move quickly toward the shore. My hair is wet, and water is running down my back. I crouch over and retch on the sandy beach.

"I almost drowned!" I gasp.

I get dressed as quickly as I can, my teeth chattering. Now all I have to do is find some dry twigs, chop up the rotten net stand from the boat for firewood, and light a fire.

I'm shivering uncontrollably. I hadn't planned on getting my head wet when I waded in. I try to light a fire, but the matches keep going out because I'm shaking so much. Eventually, I manage to get a fire started. I sit on my reindeer skin and try to get warm, rubbing my hands together. How could I have been so unlucky?

Suddenly, I don't really feel all that safe here. Is it just a *little* too quiet? I think I can hear the sound of dwarf birches breaking—or is the wind just rustling the trees?

"Hello? Is anyone there?" My voice echoes, but not a soul answers.

I'm being silly. How could I be such a coward? People who are scared in secret will never see anything supernatural—at least, that's the old belief.

The lake is calm. A few small fish are feeding close to the shore, and a pair of gray gulls are swimming nearby. Fog is rolling in with the evening air, and I can no longer see the headlands on the other side of the lake.

I light a fire by the boat and lean up against it. I'm getting a bit sleepy. I move my reindeer skin under the boat so I can take a little nap and stretch out with my hands under my head like a pillow. I hear the fire crackling and a few mosquitoes buzzing, but otherwise, it's quiet.

I stare up at the bottom of the boat. There are a lot of cracks between the planks. I'm suddenly struck by a gruesome thought: *Is this what it feels like to lie in a coffin?* Ugh, why am I getting these stupid, horrible thoughts right now when I'm all alone?

I peek out from under the boat and look at the glowing embers of the fire. It's nice and warm, and I close my eyes, listening to the sounds of the forest.

Suddenly, I hear a big splash—as if someone were wading onto the beach. Ugh, here I go scaring myself again! But that's exactly what it sounds like.

Then, I swear I can hear someone walking toward me. I hold my breath. *Is this really happening?*

Suddenly, something hits the boat so hard that even the

ground shakes. Who could have done that? I have no idea! I'm so scared I can taste blood. I don't dare move a muscle.

I feel like I'm a tiny animal terrified of being eaten by a predator. Slowly, I turn my head to see what's there, and there is a soaking-wet fishing net hanging over the boat. It's dripping with green slime, and plants from the bottom of the lake are stuck throughout. Now it feels like *I'm* stuck in the net as well!

The net is almost torn to shreds. Clearly no one has repaired it in ages. I lie under the boat, completely silent. I pray that whoever put the net on the boat won't realize that I'm there.

I can hear someone walking back and forth—and they seem angry. They kick at the fireplace, and coals fly all the way over to the boat. The embers land right in front of my face and my cheeks sting. Can they see me in my hiding place?

I'm shaking with fear, and—as quietly as I possibly can—I try to find my knife in my pocket. Imagine if that monster attacks me. What would I do?

Then, someone roars as loud as a thunderclap! It almost feels like my heart will burst out of my chest.

"Some damned person burned up my net holder! If I find them, I'll drag them to the bottom of the lake!"

I spot a pair of moccasined feet right next to the boat. The creature is standing close, but it can't see me in the dark! The moccasins are old and covered in holes, and the lake's muddy bottom has discoloured the laces. A strange scent fills my nostrils.

I realize that I've antagonized this ancient man, and now he's going to come after me! I don't want to be here anymore. I just want

to go back to my room and hide under the covers. But I'm out in the woods, a half-day's walk from the village. I don't know how I'll be able to get out from under the boat unnoticed, and besides, the net is covering it up. It feels like I'm in a prison with that horrible creature stomping back and forth out there! I'll probably die here. I shouldn't have thought about coffins before—now it's all coming true! Tears are streaming down my face. *It's going to find me!* I think.

Time passes slowly as I await my fate. Every moment over the course of my life—good and bad—seems to flash before my eyes. Is this really how my life is going to end, here on the lakeshore, hidden beneath an upside-down coffin?

Dawn finally breaks, and the fog starts burning off with the first sunbeams. I can see the old man tossing the slimy net over his shoulder and splashing into the lake. The sand is wet and dark wherever he's been walking, with glossy beetles crawling in his footsteps. I look at the old man's back. Only his skeleton is visible through the worn-out clothes. He's just bones!

He disappears back into the depths in a sea of bubbles.

Will he come back? I wonder. *Did I have a nightmare, or have I gone crazy?*

I stay lying there until it starts warming up, and then I lift the boat and creep out. I look around like a scared little animal, shaking like a leaf. I don't dare look back as I run home as fast as I can.

I left my backpack by the fireplace and my reindeer skin under the boat, but I never dared return to that awful place to retrieve my things.

Now I know why no one ever fished in that lake. The sun's rays reached all the way down to the bottom, glittering over brown sand

and stones in the water. Right where it started getting deeper, waves had scattered the skeleton of some poor man. Minnows and water beetles darted in and out through the skull's black eye sockets, and its chalk-white teeth seemed to be biting into the dark lakebed, lurking, waiting.

Glossary

divination
> finding out hidden knowledge or predicting the future, usually through supernatural powers.

fjord
> a long, narrow body of water with cliffs, mountains, or ridges on either side.

moor
> an area with wet, spongy ground.

reindeer
> caribou; while reindeer and caribou are the same species, they are referred to as "reindeer" in northern Europe and Asia, and "caribou" in North America. In Europe and Asia, "reindeer" refers to both wild and domestic members of the species. In North America, "caribou" refers to the wild members of the species, and "reindeer" refers to the domestic ones.

Glossary of North Sámi Terms

áhkku (ah-koo)
> grandmother

ájján (ahd-jahn)
> old man

Cálmmo (chahl-moh)
> a common name for a dog in Norway, and also a play on the North Sámi word for "eyes" (*almmit*)

muodd'áddjá (moo-ohd ad-jah)
> word used for "bear" in North Sámi. The word directly translates to "old man with fur." In the past, people were afraid that using the word for bear would make a bear come to them, so they made up other names for it.

ráimmahallan
(rah-ee-mah-hah-lahn)
> loosely translates to "being scared of ghosts"

About the Author

Edel Marit Gaino was born in 1972 and grew up in the small Sámi village of Láhpoluoppal in northern Norway. In her writing, she likes to showcase the traditional Sámi storytelling tradition, which is also the way she likes telling stories to children. Sámi culture and the Sámi language are the subjects closest to her heart.

About the Illustrator

From his early days of reading sci-fi and fantasy books, **Toma Feizo Gas** has been fascinated with the dramatic scenes portrayed on the covers of those books. This began his lifelong love affair with telling stories through pictures. Today, Toma's key influence remains the people in these stories, the motives that drive us, and the decisions that shape us, propelling him to craft bold visual statements and contrast in his own art. As a career illustrator, his work can be found gracing the pages and covers of titles such as *Dungeons & Dragons*, *Pathfinder*, *Star Wars*, and *Mutant Chronicles* role-playing games, as well as several upcoming fantasy novel series.

About the Translators

Olivia Lasky is an Oslo-based translator who focuses on Norwegian and North Sámi to English literary translations. Originally from Coast Miwok land in the San Francisco Bay Area, she received a Master of Arts in Scandinavian Studies with a focus on Sámi from the University of Wisconsin–Madison, and Bachelors of Arts in Scandinavian Studies and English Literature from the University of California–Berkeley. One of her main goals as a translator is to bring more Sámi voices to a wider English-speaking audience.

Lea Simma was born in 1989 and was raised in the Lávnnjitvuopmi Sámi reindeer herding area. She now lives in Dálvvadis/Jokkmokk. She has always advocated for Sámi rights and has been active in Sámi organizations both nationally and internationally. She has translated texts, books, films, and TV shows. She works at Tjállegoahte – Författarcentrum Sápmi, an organization that promotes Sámi literature.